Disney · PIXAR

INSIDE OUT

Disney · PIXAR

INSIDE OUT 2

Random House New York

Published in the United States by Random House Children's Books,
a division of Penguin Random House LLC, 1745 Broadway, New York, NY
10019, and in Canada by Penguin Random House Canada Limited, Toronto,
in conjunction with Disney Enterprises, Inc. RH Graphic with the book
design is a trademark of Penguin Random House LLC. Random House and
the colophon are registered trademarks of Penguin Random House LLC.

rhcbooks.com

ISBN 978-0-7364-4449-1 (trade) — ISBN 978-0-7364-4450-7 (ebook)

Printed in the United States of America

10 9 8 7 6 5 4 3 2 1

DISNEP · PIXAR

INSIDE OUT

DISNEP · PIXAR

INSIDE OUT 2

Random House 🏠 New York

MEET *the* CHARACTERS

JOY

Always a **CHEERFUL OPTIMIST,** Joy will do whatever it takes to make sure that her girl, Riley, has an awesome life. Working with fellow Emotions Anger, Disgust, Fear, and Sadness, Joy has her tried-and-true plans to keep Riley happy and protect her Sense of Self. But all that changes the day some new Emotions show up!

ANGER

Though he can be pretty hot-headed and **EXPLOSIVE,** Anger is willing to risk anything and take any chances, all to get the very best for Riley.

DISGUST

Now that Riley is a teenager, Disgust's role is even more important. Disgust is in charge of knowing what's **COOL** and what isn't, and she isn't afraid to point out when something is totally **CRINGE**.

FEAR

Fear may be **OVERPROTECTIVE** of Riley, but that's only because he's always terrified. Fear's job is to keep Riley as **SAFE** as he can, so he's always on the lookout for danger. But Fear can't possibly be prepared for what happens when the new Emotions arrive.

SADNESS

Besides being pretty sad, Sadness is not very confident in herself, but Joy knows that Sadness **HAS WHAT IT TAKES** to help make Riley's life amazing. Constantly concerned that she might do something to ruin everything, Sadness must learn to overcome her self-doubt when the new Emotions appear!

MEET *the* CHARACTERS

ANXIETY

Anxiety is **NERVOUS** and worried, to say the least. Always thinking ten steps ahead, Anxiety has sworn to be prepared for every possible pitfall in Riley's life, to make sure she fits in with her peers and never makes a mistake . . . no matter what Anxiety has to do to make it happen.

EMBARRASSMENT

Embarrassment is **BIG, AWKWARD,** very **SHY**, and clumsy, but he has a big heart. While he can't turn invisible, Embarrassment does the next best thing to make himself feel less noticed: he pulls the drawstring on his hoodie tight, closing it around his face. It kind of works. . . .

ENVY

SMALL but **MIGHTY**, Envy helps Riley figure out what she wants. Unfortunately, Envy wants a lot and doesn't always appreciate what Riley already has! When Envy sets her sights on Riley becoming a part of the varsity hockey team, she won't let Riley's best friends, Bree and Grace, get in the way.

ENNUI

Ennui prefers to stay put on her couch in Headquarters. She's too **BORED** to get up, so she drives the console by using an app on her phone. Ennui doesn't care about anything, which is valuable to teenage Riley, who's trying to appear **COOL** to her friends.

MEET the CHARACTERS

RILEY

Riley is now thirteen and navigating all the ups and downs of being a teenager! Excited to attend hockey camp with her best friends, Bree and Grace, Riley hopes they will get a spot on the Fire Hawks team in school next year! But things take a turn when Riley finds out that she and her besties won't be going to the same school. . . .

VALENTINA

The varsity captain of the Fire Hawks hockey team, Valentina "Val" Ortiz, is probably the coolest girl Riley has ever met. She always seems to know exactly what to do or say, and she's incredibly kind and supportive. She's popular and confident, but deep down, she has her own insecurities, too.

BREE AND GRACE

Riley's best friends, Bree and Grace, love hockey almost as much as Riley does! They are thrilled to go to hockey camp together. But how will not going to the same school next year affect their friendship?

8

I'M SADNESS.

OH, HELLO. I'M JOY.

AND THAT WAS JUST THE BEGINNING.

THAT'S FEAR.

AHH! LOOK OUT! NO!

HE'S REALLY GOOD AT KEEPING RILEY SAFE.

THIS IS DISGUST.

THAT IS NOT BRIGHTLY COLORED OR SHAPED LIKE A DINOSAUR. HOLD ON...IT'S BROCCOLI!

SHE KEEPS RILEY FROM BEING POISONED. PHYSICALLY AND SOCIALLY.

AND THAT'S ANGER.

WAIT. DID DAD JUST SAY WE COULDN'T HAVE DESSERT?

HE CARES VERY DEEPLY ABOUT THINGS BEING FAIR.

OH, AN AIRPLANE. WE GOT AN AIRPLANE, EVERYBODY!

AND YOU'VE MET SADNESS. SHE, WELL...I'M NOT SURE WHAT SHE DOES. SHE'S GOOD, WE'RE GOOD. IT'S ALL GREAT!

ANYWAY, THESE ARE RILEY'S MEMORIES...

...AND THEY'RE MOSTLY HAPPY, YOU'LL NOTICE, NOT TO BRAG.

BUT THE *REALLY* IMPORTANT ONES ARE OVER HERE. I DON'T WANT TO GET TOO TECHNICAL, BUT THESE ARE CALLED *CORE MEMORIES.*

EACH ONE CAME FROM A SUPER-IMPORTANT TIME IN RILEY'S LIFE. LIKE WHEN SHE FIRST SCORED A GOAL. THAT WAS SO AMAZING....

AND EACH CORE MEMORY POWERS A DIFFERENT ASPECT OF RILEY'S PERSONALITY....

RRRRR

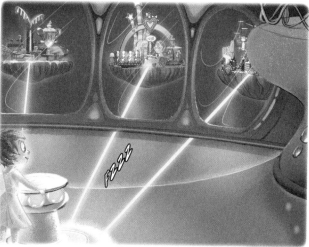

FZZZ

HONESTY ISLAND.

HOCKEY ISLAND.

FRIENDSHIP ISLAND.

GOOFBALL ISLAND.

AND OF COURSE FAMILY ISLAND.

GOOFBALL ISLAND IS MY PERSONAL FAVORITE.

BEEP BOOM SPLOSH KLANG VRRR

YUP, GOOFBALL IS THE BEST!

HAHAHA!

COME BACK HERE, YOU LITTLE MONKEY!

THE ISLANDS OF PERSONALITY ARE WHAT MAKE RILEY...RILEY!

GOOD NIGHT, KIDDO.

GOOD NIGHT, DAD.

AND... WE'RE OUT! ANOTHER PERFECT DAY!

LET'S GET THOSE MEMORIES DOWN TO LONG TERM.

CLACK

AND THAT'S IT. WE LOVE OUR GIRL. SHE'S GOT GREAT FRIENDS AND A GREAT HOUSE. THINGS COULDN'T BE BETTER.

FFFSSSHHHP

AFTER ALL, RILEY'S ELEVEN NOW. WHAT COULD HAPPEN?

WHA--

AIIIIGHH!!!

A MOVING VAN TAKES ALL OF RILEY'S BELONGINGS AWAY AND SHE TRAVELS ACROSS THE COUNTRY WITH HER PARENTS, FROM MINNESOTA...

...TO SAN FRANCISCO, CALIFORNIA!

HEY, LOOK! THE GOLDEN GATE BRIDGE! ISN'T THAT GREAT?!

WE'RE ALMOST TO OUR NEW HOUSE, RILEY!

BUT THE NEW HOME IS NOT SO GREAT....

WE'RE SUPPOSED TO LIVE HERE?

DO WE HAVE TO?

I'M TELLING YOU, IT SMELLS LIKE SOMETHING DIED IN HERE.

CAN YOU DIE FROM MOVING?

14

I'M SORRY. SOMETHING'S WRONG WITH ME. I KEEP MAKING MISTAKES LIKE THAT. I'M AWFUL...AND ANNOYING...

WELL...UH... YOU CAN'T FOCUS ON WHAT'S GOING WRONG. THERE'S ALWAYS A WAY TO TURN THINGS AROUND, TO FIND THE FUN.

FIND THE FUN... I DON'T KNOW HOW TO DO THAT....

OKAY, WELL... TRY TO THINK OF SOMETHING FUNNY.

WHAT ABOUT THAT TIME WITH MEG, WHEN RILEY LAUGHED SO HARD MILK CAME OUT OF HER NOSE?

YEAH. THAT HURT. IT FELT LIKE FIRE. OOH, IT WAS AWFUL.

YOU KNOW WHAT? LET'S THINK ABOUT SOMETHING ELSE. HOW ABOUT WE READ SOME MIND MANUALS, HUH? SOUNDS FUN!

?

MEMORIES OF ANGER, FEAR AND DISGUST ARE BEING CREATED ONE AFTER THE OTHER....

UGH...

WHIRR

WHERE'S DAD?

ON THE PHONE. THIS NEW VENTURE IS KEEPING HIM PRETTY BUSY.

YOUR DAD'S A LITTLE STRESSED--YOU KNOW, ABOUT GETTING HIS NEW COMPANY UP AND RUNNING....

I GUESS ALL I REALLY WANT TO SAY IS, THANK YOU.

!

HUH?

THROUGH ALL THIS CONFUSION YOU'VE STAYED...WELL, YOU'VE STAYED OUR HAPPY GIRL. AND IF YOU AND I CAN KEEP SMILING, IT WOULD BE A BIG HELP TO YOUR DAD.

YEAH, SURE.

WELL, YOU CAN'T ARGUE WITH MOM. "HAPPY" IT IS.

TEAM HAPPY! SOUNDS GREAT!

I'M TOTALLY BEHIND YOU, JOY.

LOOKS LIKE WE'RE GOING INTO *REM*. SLEEP WELL, TEAM HAPPY!

19

20

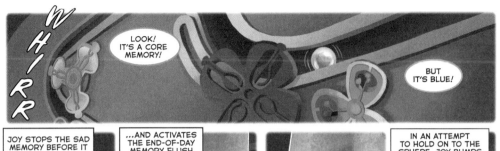

...AND ACTIVATES THE END-OF-DAY MEMORY FLUSH TUBE TO VACUUM IT UP!

JOY STOPS THE SAD MEMORY BEFORE IT REACHES THE CORE MEMORY HOLDER...

IN AN ATTEMPT TO HOLD ON TO THE SPHERE, JOY BUMPS AGAINST THE CORE MEMORY HOLDER....

AND JUST LIKE THAT, THE PERSONALITY ISLANDS GO DARK!

JOY COLLECTS ALL THE CORE MEMORIES, BUT...

NO! NO! NO!

NO!

NOOOO!

CAN I SAY THAT CURSE WORD NOW?

THANK YOU, RILEY. I KNOW IT CAN BE TOUGH MOVING TO A NEW PLACE, BUT WE'RE HAPPY TO HAVE YOU HERE.

LATER THAT EVENING, RILEY IS HAVING DINNER WITH MOM AND DAD....

I FOUND A JUNIOR HOCKEY LEAGUE RIGHT HERE IN SAN FRANCISCO. AND GET THIS...TRYOUTS ARE TOMORROW AFTER SCHOOL. WHAT LUCK, RIGHT?

HOCKEY?

UH-OH. WHAT DO WE DO?

YOU PRETEND TO BE JOY!

WON'T IT BE GREAT TO BE BACK OUT ON THE ICE?

OH YEAH, THAT SOUNDS *FANTASTIC.*

WHAT WAS THAT? THAT WASN'T ANYTHING LIKE JOY.

UH, BECAUSE I'M *NOT* JOY.

THE SITUATION GETS WORSE WHEN ANGER TAKES CONTROL....

RILEY, IS EVERYTHING OKAY?

RILEY, I DO *NOT* LIKE THIS NEW ATTITUDE.

OH, I'LL SHOW YOU ATTITUDE, OLD MAN*!*

WHAT IS YOUR PROBLEM? JUST LEAVE ME ALONE!

THAT IS IT*!* GO TO YOUR ROOM! NOW*!*

26

HEY...

SO...THINGS GOT A LITTLE OUT OF HAND DOWNSTAIRS. YOU WANT TO TALK ABOUT IT?

COME ON, WHERE'S MY HAPPY GIRL? MONKEY... OO! OO! OOO!

OHHH! HE'S TRYING TO START UP GOOFBALL!

BUT GOOFBALL ISLAND WON'T WORK....

IT BREAKS DOWN AND CRUMBLES!

RRRRRUMBLE

AHHHH!

27

I GET IT, YOU NEED SOME ALONE TIME. WE'LL TALK LATER.

WE LOST GOOFBALL ISLAND. THAT MEANS SHE CAN LOSE FRIENDSHIP, AND HOCKEY, AND HONESTY, AND FAMILY. YOU CAN FIX THIS, RIGHT, JOY?

I... I DON'T KNOW.

BUT WE HAVE TO TRY.

AT THAT MOMENT THE SKY DARKENS....

RILEY'S GONE TO SLEEP...

!

...WHICH IS A GOOD THING! BECAUSE NOTHING ELSE BAD CAN HAPPEN WHILE SHE'S ASLEEP, AND WE'LL BE BACK TO HEADQUARTERS BEFORE SHE WAKES UP.

WE'LL JUST GO ACROSS FRIENDSHIP ISLAND....

28

WE'LL NEVER MAKE IT... OHHHH...

NO! NO! NO! DON'T OBSESS OVER THE WEIGHT OF LIFE'S PROBLEMS!

WE'LL JUST HAVE TO GO AROUND!

WAIT! JOY, YOU COULD GET LOST IN THERE! THAT'S LONG-TERM MEMORY...AN ENDLESS WARREN OF CORRIDORS AND SHELVES. I READ ABOUT IT IN THE MANUAL.

THE MANUAL!

SO YOU KNOW THE WAY BACK TO HEADQUARTERS! YOU ARE MY MAP!

OKAY! LET'S GO! LEAD ON, MIND MAP! SHOW ME WHERE WE'RE GOING!

OKAY! ONLY...I'M TOO SAD TO WALK. JUST GIVE ME A FEW... HOURS.

JOY HAS NO CHOICE BUT TO DRAG SADNESS....

RILEY'S AWAKE!

RILEY CHATS WITH HER BEST FRIEND, MEG....

DO YOU LIKE IT THERE?

YEAH. IT'S GOOD.... WHAT HAPPENED WITH THE PLAYOFFS?

WE WON THE FIRST GAME. COACH SAYS WE MIGHT ACTUALLY GO TO THE FINALS THIS YEAR. OH, AND WE'VE GOT THIS NEW GIRL ON THE TEAM. SHE'S SO COOL.

A NEW GIRL? MEG HAS A NEW FRIEND ALREADY?!

GRRRRRRRRR!

HEY, HEY, WE DO NOT WANT TO LOSE ANY MORE ISLANDS HERE, GUYS!

WE CAN PASS THE PUCK TO EACH OTHER WITHOUT EVEN LOOKING. IT'S LIKE MIND READING!

YOU LIKE TO READ MINDS, MEG? I GOT SOMETHING FOR YOU TO READ!

I GOTTA GO.

WHAT?

I GOTTA GO.

BAM

34

INSIDE RILEY'S MIND, ANOTHER ISLAND CRUMBLES....

RRRRUMBLE

OH NO... NO, SHE LOVES HOCKEY....

BING BONG, WE HAVE TO GET TO THAT STATION.

SURE THING. THIS WAY, JUST PAST THE...

⌐GASP!⌐ MY ROCKET! WAIT!

RILEY AND I, WE'RE STILL USING THAT ROCKET! IT STILL HAS SOME SONG POWER LEFT!

36

NO! YOU CAN'T TAKE MY ROCKET TO THE DUMP! RILEY AND I ARE GOING TO THE MOON!

RILEY CAN I BE DONE WITH ME.

HEY, IT'S GOING TO BE OKAY! WE CAN FIX THIS! WE JUST NEED TO GET BACK TO HEADQUARTERS. WHICH WAY TO THE TRAIN STATION?

I HAD A WHOLE TRIP PLANNED FOR US.

I'M SORRY THEY TOOK YOUR ROCKET. THEY TOOK SOMETHING THAT YOU LOVED. IT'S GONE... FOREVER....

SADNESS, DON'T MAKE HIM FEEL WORSE.

IT'S ALL I HAD LEFT OF RILEY.

I BET YOU AND RILEY HAD GREAT ADVENTURES.

THEY WERE WONDERFU ONCE WE FLEW BAC IN TIME... WE HAD BREAKFA TWICE TH DAY!

THAT SOUNDS AMAZING. I BET RILEY LIKED IT.

OH, SHE DID.... WE WERE BEST FRIENDS....

YEAH. IT'S SAD.

I'M OKAY NOW.

C'MON, THE TRAIN STATION IS THIS WAY!

?!

HOW DID YOU DO THAT?

OH, I DON'T KNOW. HE WAS SAD, SO I LISTENED TO WHAT--

AND FINALLY, JOY, SADNESS AND BING BONG REACH THE TRAIN OF THOUGHT!

WE MADE IT! WE'RE FINALLY GOING TO GET HOME!

BACK IN HER BEDROOM, RILEY IS STILL AWAKE....

ON A SCALE OF ONE TO TEN, I GIVE THIS DAY AN F.

WHY DON'T WE QUIT STANDING AROUND AND DO SOMETHING.

LIKE WHAT, GENIUS?

LIKE THIS!

WHAT IS IT?

OH, NOTHING... JUST THE BEST IDEA EVER.

WHAT?

ALL THE GOOD CORE MEMORIES WERE MADE IN MINNESOTA. ERGO, WE GO BACK TO MINNESOTA AND MAKE MORE!

YOU CAN'T BE SERIOUS.

HEY. OUR LIFE WAS PERFECT UNTIL MOM AND DAD DECIDED TO MOVE TO SAN FRAN STINKTOWN.

WAIT, HOLD ON... SHOULDN'T WE JUST SLEEP ON THIS OR SOMETHING?

FINE. LET'S SLEEP ON IT.

BECAUSE I'M SURE JOLLY FUN-FILLED TIMES ARE JUST AROUND THE CORNER....

THE TRAIN OF THOUGHT STOPS. IT DOESN'T RUN WHILE RILEY IS ASLEEP....

WE'RE STUCK HERE UNTIL MORNING?

WE CAN'T WAIT THAT LONG!

HOW ABOUT WE WAKE HER UP?

SHORTLY AFTER, AT DREAM PRODUCTIONS...

OKAY, HOW ARE WE GONNA WAKE HER UP?

WELL, SHE WAKES UP SOMETIMES WHEN SHE HAS A SCARY DREAM. WE COULD SCARE HER.

SCARE HER? NO, NO, SHE'S BEEN THROUGH ENOUGH ALREADY.

WE'RE GONNA MAKE RILEY SO HAPPY THAT SHE'LL WAKE UP WITH EXHILARATION! PUT THIS ON....

DON'T LET ANYTHING HAPPEN TO THESE.

GOT IT!

40

AT HEADQUARTERS, FEAR IS ON DREAM DUTY....

EW, LOOK! HER TEETH ARE FALLING OUT!

TEETH FALLING OUT... I'M USED TO THAT ONE.

SUDDENLY...

BARK! BARK! BARK!

WHAT IS GOING ON?

SADNESS, WHAT ARE YOU DOING?! COME BACK HERE!

RIIIIP

IT'S JUST A DREAM! IT'S JUST A DREAM!

SADNESS! YOU ARE RUINING THIS DREAM! YOU'RE SCARING HER!

BUT LOOK...

ASLEEP

ASLEEP   AWAKE

...IT'S WORKING!

BUT...

THEY ARE NOT PART OF THIS DREAM!! GET THEM!

JOY AND SADNESS MANAGE TO ESCAPE...

...WHILE BING BONG IS ARRESTED AND TAKEN TO THE SUBCONSCIOUS.

THERE GO THE CORE MEMORIES...

I CAN'T GO IN THERE! I'M SCARED OF THE DARK! PLEASE!

COME ON...

I DON'T LIKE IT HERE. IT'S WHERE THEY KEEP RILEY'S DARKEST FEARS.

THIS IS THE HOME OF BROCCOLI, THE STAIRS TO THE BASEMENT, GRANDMA'S VACUUM CLEANER...

...AND JANGLES, THE BIRTHDAY CLOWN!

JOY?

BING BONG!

MEANWHILE, AT HEADQUARTERS...

TIME TO TAKE ACTION.

CLICK

SHE TOOK IT. THERE'S NO TURNING BACK.

HOW'RE WE GONNA GET TO MINNESOTA FROM HERE?

WE'RE TAKING THE BUS. THERE'S ONE LEAVING TOMORROW.

A TICKET COSTS MONEY. HOW DO WE GET MONEY?

MOM'S PURSE.

÷GASP!÷ YOU WOULDN'T!

MOM AND DAD GOT US INTO THIS MESS. THEY CAN PAY TO GET US OUT.

AS SOON AS RILEY TAKES THE CREDIT CARD...

...HONESTY ISLAND CRUMBLES!

RRRRRRUMBLE

AND THE TRAIN OF THOUGHT CRASHES. JOY, SADNESS AND BING BONG JUMP OUT JUST BEFORE IT SLIDES OFF THE CLIFF.

CRASH

THAT WAS OUR WAY HOME! WE LOST ANOTHER ISLAND....WHAT IS HAPPENING?

HAVEN'T YOU HEARD?

RILEY IS RUNNING AWAY!

WHAT?!

JOY, IF WE HURRY, WE CAN STILL STOP HER.

FAMILY ISLAND...

LET'S GO!

THE NEXT MORNING RILEY PRETENDS SHE'S GOING TO SCHOOL....

HAVE A GREAT DAY, SWEETHEART.

JOY! IT'S TOO DANGEROUS! WE WON'T MAKE IT IN TIME!

BUT THAT'S OUR ONLY WAY BACK!

A BIG SHELF COLLAPSES AND A RECALL TUBE IS EXPOSED....

A RECALL TUBE!

WE CAN GET RECALLED!

WHOA! SADNESS!

FZZZZ

STOP! YOU'RE HURTING RILEY!

OH NO! I DID IT AGAIN!

IF YOU GET IN HERE, THESE CORE MEMORIES WILL GET SAD.

JOY?

I'M SORRY! RILEY NEEDS TO BE HAPPY.

WOOOOH

THE RUMBLING BREAKS THE TUBE APART...

RRRRRRUMBLE

...AND THE CLIFFSIDE CRUMBLES AWAY.

JOY!

STUCK IN THE MEMORY DUMP, JOY AND BING BONG ARE DESTINED TO BE FORGOTTEN....

I JUST WANTED RILEY TO BE HAPPY. AND NOW...

?

THE MEMORY TURNS BLUE AND JOY REMEMBERS WHAT SADNESS SAID ABOUT THAT DAY....

"IT WAS THE DAY THE PRAIRIE DOGS LOST THE BIG PLAYOFF GAME. RILEY MISSED THE WINNING SHOT. SHE FELT AWFUL. SHE WANTED TO QUIT."

MOM AND DAD... THE TEAM...THEY CAME TO HELP BECAUSE OF SADNESS!

WE HAVE TO GET BACK UP THERE!

JOY, WE'RE STUCK DOWN HERE. WE MIGHT AS WELL BE ON ANOTHER PLANET.

ANOTHER PLANET!

♫ WHO'S YOUR FRIEND WHO LIKES TO PLAY? BING BONG, BING BONG! ♪

!

USING BING BONG'S ROCKET WAGON...

♫ WHO'S THE BEST IN EVERY WAY AND WANTS TO SING THIS SONG TO SAY... WHO'S YOUR FRIEND WHO LIKES TO PLAY? BING BONG, BING BONG! ♫

FWOOOO

...JOY AND BING BONG TRY TO GET OUT OF THE MEMORY DUMP.

FWOOOO

THUMP

CRASH

AFTER TWO FAILED ATTEMPTS...

FWOOOO

♫ WHO'S THE BEST IN EVERY WAY AND WANTS TO SING THIS SONG TO SAY... WHO'S YOUR FRIEND WHO LIKES TO PLAY? BING BONG, BING BONG! ♫

WOO-HOO! BING BONG, WE DID IT! WE--

INSIDE RILEY'S HEAD, SADNESS IS FLOATING AWAY...

SADNESS! WAIT!

JUST LET ME GO! RILEY'S BETTER OFF WITHOUT ME. I ONLY MAKE EVERYTHING WORSE.

BUT JOY KNOWS WHAT TO DO....

DID YOU MEAN WHAT YOU SAID BEFORE?

I WOULD DIE FOR RILEY!

TIME TO PROVE IT!

USING THE IMAGINARY BOYFRIENDS AS A TOWER, JOY FALLS ONTO FAMILY ISLAND...

...BOUNCES OFF A TRAMPOLINE THERE...

BOING

...GRABS ON TO SADNESS...

GOTCHA!

...AND THEY BOTH GO BACK TOWARD HEADQUARTERS!

THEY MAKE THEIR WAY INSIDE....

THANK GOODNESS YOU'RE BACK!

SADNESS, IT'S UP TO YOU NOW. RILEY NEEDS YOU.

OKAY.

CLACK

WAIT! STOP! I WANNA GET OFF!

RILEY, THERE YOU ARE! THANK GOODNESS!

OH, WE WERE WORRIED SICK! WHERE HAVE YOU BEEN? IT'S SO LATE....

I KNOW YOU DON'T WANT ME TO, BUT...I MISS HOME. I MISS MINNESOTA.

YOU NEED ME TO BE HAPPY, BUT...I WANT MY OLD FRIENDS, AND MY HOCKEY TEAM.... I WANNA GO HOME. PLEASE DON'T BE MAD.

OH, SWEETIE.

WE'RE NOT MAD. YOU KNOW WHAT? I MISS MINNESOTA, TOO. I MISS THE WOODS WHERE WE TOOK HIKES.

AND THE BACKYARD WHERE YOU USED TO PLAY.

SPRING LAKE, WHERE YOU LEARNED TO SKATE.

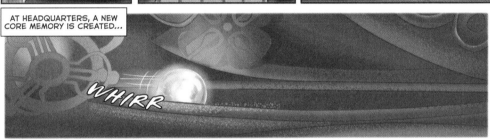
AT HEADQUARTERS, A NEW CORE MEMORY IS CREATED...

WHIRR

...AND JOY AND SADNESS FINALLY BECOME A TEAM.

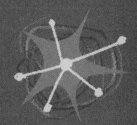

Graphic Novel

SCRIPT ADAPTATION
ALESSANDRO FERRARI

LAYOUT
MASSIMILIANO NARCISO

PENCIL
ARIANNA REA, ANDREA GREPPI,
ANDREA SCOPPETTA, FEDERICO MANCUSO

PAINT
ANDREA CAGOL, CRISTINA TONIOLO, ANTONIA EMANUELA ANGRISANI,
SARA SPANO, MASSIMO ROCCA, PATRIZIA ZANGRILLI

ARTIST COORDINATION
TOMATOFARM

EDITORIAL PAGES:
CO-D S.R.L. — MILANO

PRE-PRESS
EDIZIONI BD S.R.L.

SPECIAL THANKS
CAITLIN KENNEDY, VALERIE LAPOINTE, SCOTT TILLEY,
LAURA UYEDA, SAMANTHA WILSON

60

AHHH!!! LOOK OUT!!!

AND THAT'S *FEAR*, KEEPING RILEY ON HER TOES!

"OH MY GOSH! THAT MOUTH GUARD IS NOT OURS! *THAT'S SO GROSS!*"

AND THAT, FOLKS, IS THE INFAMOUS *DISGUST!* GLAD TO HAVE HER ON OUR TEAM!

YEAH, YOU'RE WELCOME.

GO, RILEY!

RILEY, RILEY, OVER HERE! BIG SMILE! YOU GOT THIS, SWEETHEART!

THWACK

AND BRINGING UP THE REAR--YOU KNOW HER, YOU LOVE HER--THE ONE, THE ONLY...*SADNESS* IS IN THE HOUSE!

OH, WE GOT A PENALTY.

OKAY, LET ME CATCH YOU UP. RILEY IS OFFICIALLY A TEENAGER NOW! AND YOU KNOW WHAT THAT MEANS: *CHANGES*. BIG ONES.

AS RILEY GROWS UP, THE CONSOLE IN HEADQUARTERS KEEPS EXPANDING, TOO!

RILEY IS STILL EXCEPTIONAL, BECAUSE SHE'S SMART AND REALLY KIND, NICE TO STRAY CATS...I MEAN, COME ON!

RILEY'S *PERSONALITY ISLANDS* ARE STILL GOING STRONG.

HOCKEY ISLAND

FRIENDSHIP ISLAND

FAMILY ISLAND

GOOFBALL ISLAND

THAT BIG ONE IS *FRIENDSHIP ISLAND*. ISN'T IT AMAZING?

WE LOVE OUR NEW BFFS, BREE AND GRACE.

WE REALIZED HER ISLANDS AREN'T THE ONLY THINGS MADE BY MEMORIES. WAY DOWN AT THE ROOT LEVEL, THESE MEMORIES WERE ALSO CREATING *BELIEFS*.

"IF YOU DON'T RUN UP THE BASEMENT STAIRS REALLY FAST, A HAND WILL GRAB YOUR ANKLE."

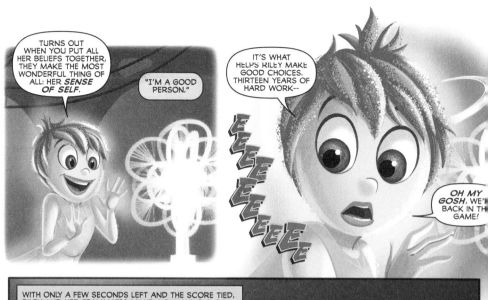

TURNS OUT WHEN YOU PUT ALL HER BELIEFS TOGETHER, THEY MAKE THE MOST WONDERFUL THING OF ALL: HER *SENSE OF SELF.*

"I'M A GOOD PERSON."

IT'S WHAT HELPS RILEY MAKE GOOD CHOICES. THIRTEEN YEARS OF HARD WORK--

OH MY *GOSH*, WE'[RE] BACK IN TH[E] GAME!

WITH ONLY A FEW SECONDS LEFT AND THE SCORE TIED, RILEY AND HER TEAMMATES MAKE A PLAN. THE CLOCK COUNTS DOWN, AND THANKS TO SOME FANCY TEAMWORK, THE FOGHORNS *WIN* THE CHAMPIONSHIP...

...AND RILEY'S *SENSE OF SELF* GLOWS.

LATER, AS RILEY AND HER FRIENDS CELEBRATE...

HEY, GIRLS! CONGRATULATIONS ON YOUR WIN!

IT'S *COACH ROBERTS!* SHE'S THE HIGH SCHOOL COACH!

64

THOSE FIRE HAWKS WILL BE *LUCKY* TO HAVE YOU!

EXACTLY! MOM AND DAD GET IT.

EVENTUALLY, RILEY DRIFTS OFF TO SLEEP.

OH, RILEY'S SO HARD ON HERSELF.

WE CAN MAKE EVERYTHING EASIER!

BEHOLD! MY SUPER-HIGH-TECH RILEY PROTECTION SYSTEM.

THIS IS FOR ALL THOSE MEMORIES THAT BELONG IN THE *BACK OF THE MIND*. LIKE THIS PENALTY ONE. IT'S WEIGHING ON HER, SO LET'S LIGHTEN THE LOAD.

A ONE-WAY EXPRESSWAY TO "WE'RE NOT GONNA THINK ABOUT THAT RIGHT NOW!"

THE EMOTIONS LOVE JOY'S NEW SYSTEM AND HELP GET RID OF *MORE* BAD MEMORIES!

OH, HERE'S ONE WHERE RILEY WAVED AT A GUY WHO WAS ACTUALLY WAVING AT A GIRL BEHIND HER.

HERE'S WHEN SHE FORGOT THAT GIRL'S NAME.

JOY LOADS MORE BAD MEMORIES INTO THE SYSTEM AND SENDS THEM AWAY!

WE KEEP THE BEST AND TOSS THE REST!

LATER JOY HOLDS THE MEMORY OF TODAY'S CHAMPIONSHIP WIN...

ARE YOU TAKING THAT WHERE I THINK YOU'RE TAKING THAT?

WANNA COME THIS TIME?

YOU'RE THE ONLY ONE WHO HASN'T BEEN TO THE *BELIEF SYSTEM*.

I DON'T WANT TO MESS IT UP OR BREAK IT OR ANYTHING.

YOU WON'T HURT IT. I PROMISE.

JOY TAKES SADNESS TO RILEY'S BELIEF SYSTEM FAR BELOW HEADQUARTERS AND PLUCKS ONE OF HER BELIEF STRINGS.

"MOM AND DAD ARE PROUD OF ME."

AN OLDIE BUT A GOODIE.

NOW SADNESS TRIES....

"I'M KIND."

AWWWW. THAT'S NICE.

"I'M STRONG."

"I'M BRAVE."

"I'M A REALLY GOOD FRIEND."

JOY PLUCKS A BELIEF THAT HAS JUST GROWN FROM RILEY'S CHAMPIONSHIP WIN MEMORY....

AND ALL THESE BELIEFS COME TOGETHER TO MAKE *OUR* RILEY.

"I'M A WINNER."

"I'M A GOOD PERSON."

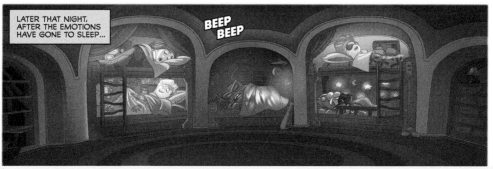

LATER THAT NIGHT, AFTER THE EMOTIONS HAVE GONE TO SLEEP...

BEEP BEEP

66

BEEP BEEP

WHAT THE HECK IS *THAT*?

MOMENTS LATER, JOY LOOKS FOR THE SOURCE OF THE SOUND....

BEEP BEEP

IT'S THE *POOBERTY* ALARM?

SUDDENLY...

BEEEEEEEEEEEP

AH! IT'S THE APOCALYPSE!

TURN THAT OFF! WHAT IS HAPPENING?

THINKING FAST, JOY SENDS THE ALARM TO THE BACK OF THE MIND!

WHOOSH

WHEW! PROBLEM SOLVED.

NOT QUITE!

CRASH

AAAHHH!

LET THE PROFESSIONAL HANDLE THIS.

I'M TOO GROSS TO GO TO CAMP OR ANYWHERE EVER AGAIN!

OH YEAH, THIS IS TOTALLY BROKEN.

AT LAST, RILEY AND HER FRIENDS HEAD TO HOCKEY CAMP....

WE'RE GONNA HAVE SO MUCH FUN!

UNTIL WE CAN FIGURE THIS OUT, NOBODY TOUCH THE CONSOLE UNLESS YOU REALLY NEED TO!

YOU GUYS! I'M SO PSYCHED!

I KNOW! HOW GREAT IS *NEXT YEAR* GONNA BE?!

AND VAL ORTIZ IS THE CAPTAIN NOW! SHE'S SO AMAZING.

ALL WE HAVE TO DO IS BE SUPER AWESOME AT CAMP.

COACH ROBERTS WILL PUT US ON THE TEAM, AND WE'LL ALL BE FIRE HAWKS!

WAIT. WHAT WAS THAT?

WHAT WAS WHAT?

WE GOT A *LOOK*. I DON'T LIKE THIS.

COACH ROBERTS ISN'T GOING TO BE OUR COACH NEXT YEAR....

WE GOT ASSIGNED TO A DIFFERENT HIGH SCHOOL.

OH, OKAY. UM, YEAH, NO BIG DEAL.

WE CAN'T GO TO HIGH SCHOOL WITHOUT BREE AND GRACE.

WE WON'T KNOW ANYBODY!

WE'LL STILL HANG OUT.

AND WE'LL HAVE THIS WEEKEND, ONE LAST TIME PLAYING ON THE SAME TEAM.

FRIENDS ARE FOREVER, RIGHT?

YEAH. OF COURSE.

OH, THIS IS *SO SAD*.

WAIT! JUST KEEP IT TOGETHER UNTIL THEY'RE OUT OF THE CAR!

ANGER WANTS TO CORRECT VAL, BECAUSE RILEY IS FROM MINNESOTA, NOT MICHIGAN.

NO, NO, NO, NO! WE CANNOT CORRECT *VAL ORTIZ!*

ORANGE? WHO MADE THE CONSOLE *ORANGE?*

HELLO, EVERYBODY. I'M *ANXIETY.* I'M ONE OF RILEY'S NEW EMOTIONS!

WE ARE JUST SUPER JAZZED TO BE HERE.

WHAT DO YOU MEAN *"WE"?*

I'M ENVY. OOOH! LOOK AT *HER* HAIR. WE NEED HAIR LIKE THAT!

ENVY PRESSES A BUTTON ON THE CONSOLE, AND...

OH MY GOSH, I LOVE THE RED IN YOUR HAIR!

MAYBE WHEN I MAKE THE TEAM, I CAN JOIN TEAM RED HEAD, TOO! YEAH, YEAH!

SUDDENLY, RILEY BECOMES EMBARRASSED!

WHAT'S YOUR NAME, BIG FELLA?

THAT'S EMBARRASSMENT!

DO YOU WANNA COME WITH ME, ACTUALLY? YOU CAN MEET SOME OF THE OTHER FIRE HAWKS.

OOOH! THIS IS EXCITING! BUT WE CAN'T LET HER KNOW WE'RE EXCITED.

YEAH, SOUNDS GOOD.

WHAT EMOTION WAS *THAT?*

THAT'S ENNUI.

÷SIGH÷ IT'S WHAT YOU WOULD CALL "THE BOREDOM."

AS HOCKEY CAMP BEGINS, ANXIETY LAYS OUT HER PLAN...

THE NEXT THREE DAYS COULD DETERMINE THE NEXT *FOUR YEARS OF OUR LIVES.*

I THINK THAT'S OVERSTATING THINGS A BIT.

IF RILEY DOESN'T TAKE THIS CAMP SERIOUSLY AND WE GOOF OFF WITH BREE AND GRACE...

...RILEY LOOKS REALLY UNCOOL IN FRONT OF VAL.

SHE FAILS TO IMPRESS COACH, DOES NOT BECOME A FIRE HAWK...

...AND FINALLY ARRIVES AT HIGH SCHOOL. SHE HAS *NO ONE.*

SHE EATS ALONE, AND ONLY THE TEACHERS KNOW HER NAME.

LOVE THE ENERGY, BUT NONE OF THIS WILL ACTUALLY HAPPEN.

WE'RE HERE TO HAVE FUN! THESE NEXT THREE DAYS NEED TO BE ABOUT BREE AND GRACE.

RIGHT. WHATEVER YOU SAY. YOU'RE THE BOSS.

SO RILEY TAKES A SEAT IN THE LOCKER ROOM....

I WANT YOU TO MEET THE OTHER FIRE HAWKS!

HEY.

YOU WANNA SIT WITH US?

I WAS GONNA SAVE SEATS FOR MY FRIENDS, BUT THANKS ANYWAY.

OH, UH, YEAH, OKAY. NO WORRIES.

SEE? WAS THAT SO HARD?

NO, THAT DECISION'S NOT GONNA HAUNT US FOR THE REST OF OUR LIVES AT ALL.

BREE AND GRACE ARRIVE, AND THE FRIENDS GET SILLY....

SAY "AHWOOGA"!

UH, JOY...

LADIES, SETTLE DOWN. I NEED YOUR FOCUS.

WHICH MEANS NOW I'M GONNA NEED YOUR CELL PHONES. ALL OF 'EM.

YOU'RE HERE TO WORK. NOT GOOF AROUND. GOT THAT, ANDERSEN?

YES, COACH.

JOY, MAYBE, UM, I COULD HELP--

THANK YOU, NOT NOW.

COACH IS SO SERIOUS.

I KNOW, RIGHT?

OH, YOU THINK THIS IS FUNNY? WELL, YOU KNOW WHAT ELSE IS FUNNY?

SKATING LINES! NOW HIT THE ICE, LADIES!

BRAVO, JOY. SHE'S TOTALLY FITTING IN NOW.

LATER, AT THE RINK...

ALL RIGHT, LADIES! TAKE A BREATHER. THEN WE'LL DIVIDE INTO TEAMS.

THAT MICHIGAN GIRL'S OFF TO A ROUGH START.

COACH ISN'T GONNA PUT HER ON THE TEAM IF SHE CAN'T GET IT TOGETHER.

LIKE *YOU* HAD IT ALL TOGETHER WHEN *YOU* WERE A FRESHMAN?

~GROAN~

I GOT YOU, BIG GUY.

THEN RILEY FIGHTS BACK TEARS!

JOY, WHAT DO WE DO NOW?

UM, WE CAN JUST... UM--

I HAVE AN IDEA!

IF WE CAN GET VAL ON OUR SIDE, EVERYTHING WILL BE GREAT.

ANXIETY TAKES THAT IDEA AND PUTS IT IN THE CONSOLE...

...AND RILEY TAKES OFF WITH IT!

UH, VAL? I'M SO SORRY. I DIDN'T MEAN TO GET THE WHOLE TEAM SKATING LINES. I FEEL TERRIBLE.

YOU LEAD THE TEAM SO AMAZINGLY, AND I REALLY LOOK UP TO YOU, AND--

OKAY, OKAY-- THANKS.

LISTEN, COACH WAS HARD ON YOU TODAY. BUT THAT'S NOT A BAD THING. IT MEANS YOU'RE ON HER RADAR.

I'M GLAD YOU CAME TO TALK WITH ME. LET'S TRY TO BE ON THE SAME TEAM LATER, OKAY?

OH, YEAH! COOL.

GOOD JOB. WOW.

I WISH I COULD DO THAT!

AW, YOU GUYS. I'M JUST TRYING TO HELP.

GREAT JOB, ANXIETY. YOU STEPPED IN. YOU GOT RILEY BACK ON TRACK. NOW I'M READY TO STEP BACK IN.

BUT THAT WAS JUST PART ONE OF MY PLAN.

"A GOOD PLAN HAS MANY PARTS, JOY."

OKAY, LADIES, WE'RE GONNA FORM YOUR TEAMS FOR THE REST OF CAMP. TEAM ONE ON THE RIGHT, AND TEAM TWO ON THE LEFT.

COME ON, RILEY, MOVE. MOVE THOSE FEET. VAL'S ON TEAM ONE. YOU WANNA BE ON TEAM ONE. LET'S GO.

SHE MADE A PROMISE TO BREE AND GRACE. SHE'S NOT GONNA BREAK IT.

ANXIETY PULLS OUT RILEY'S SENSE OF SELF...

WHAT ARE YOU DOING?!

I DON'T MEAN TO OVERSTEP, BUT IT HAS TO BE DONE.

...AND SENDS IT TO THE BACK OF THE MIND!

STOP! NO!

I KNOW CHANGE IS SCARY, BUT WATCH.

RILEY?

WELCOME TO OUR TEAM, MICHIGAN.

WHY DID SHE DO THAT? THIS WAS OUR LAST CHANCE TO PLAY TOGETHER.

THAT IS *NOT* RILEY!

I KNOW! IT'S A *BETTER* RILEY.

A RILEY WHO WON'T BE ALONE NEXT YEAR.

WE BUILD HER A NEW *SENSE OF SELF*. A *BRAND-NEW HER!*

ANXIETY PREPARES TO TAKE THE NEW MEMORY DOWN TO THE BELIEF SYSTEM....

YOU CAN'T GO DOWN THERE WITH THAT MEMORY.

OVER MY DEAD FLAMING BODY.

HEY! WHAT DO YOU THINK YOU'RE DOING?

RILEY'S LIFE REQUIRES MORE SOPHISTICATED EMOTIONS NOW. YOU'RE JUST NOT WHAT SHE NEEDS ANYMORE, JOY.

THE MIND COPS TAKE JOY AND THE OTHERS AWAY....

YOU CAN'T JUST BOTTLE US UP!

DON'T WORRY, RILEY. YOU'RE IN GOOD HANDS.

NOW LET'S CHANGE EVERYTHING ABOUT YOU.

SOON, AT THE VAULT, WHERE ALL OF RILEY'S SECRETS ARE KEPT...

WE ARE... *SUPPRESSED EMOTIONS!*

NO! NO! *NO!* RILEY'S GONNA BE FINE. TOTALLY FINE!

HEY THERE! YOU KNOW WHAT WE CALL THAT? DENIAL. CAN *YOU* SAY "DENIAL"?

HI, FRIENDS! WELCOME! IT'S SO GOOD TO HAVE YOU HERE WITH US TODAY.

IT'S *BLOOFY!*

FROM THAT PRESCHOOL SHOW RILEY USED TO LIKE?

THAT'S *RIGHT!* AND HERE'S A LITTLE SECRET: RILEY *STILL* LIKES THE SHOW.

BLOOFY! WE'RE IN A REAL PICKLE! COULD YOU HELP US GET OUTTA HERE?!

UH-OH! WE'RE GONNA NEED YOUR HELP! CAN *YOU* FIND A WAY OUT?

WHO ARE YOU TALKING TO?!

MY FRIENDS!

OKAY. WE'RE DOOMED.

INDEED. WELCOME TO YOUR ETERNAL FATE.

LANCE SLASHBLADE?!

BUT HE'S A *VIDEO GAME CHARACTER.* WHY IS HE HERE?

I ALWAYS THOUGHT RILEY HAD A SECRET CRUSH ON HIM.

UH, WHO'S *THAT*?

OH! THAT'S RILEY'S *DEEP DARK SECRET!*

YOU DON'T WANNA KNOW.

RILEY'S SECRETS! A ROGUE EMOTION HAS TAKEN OVER HEADQUARTERS! NOW, IF YOU COULD JUST OPEN THE JAR...

MOMENTS LATER...

SMASH

NOW IT'S YOUR TURN TO HELP *US!* MY POUCH HAS JUST THE THING TO GET US OUTTA HERE.

EVERYBODY SAY, "OH, POUCHY!"

HI, EVERYBODY! I'M *POUCHY!*

POUCHY, WE NEED TO ESCAPE. DO YOU HAVE ANYTHING THAT CAN HELP US?

I HAVE LOTS OF ITEMS! WHICH ONE DO YOU THINK WILL WORK THE BEST?

A TOMATO? A FROG? OR...*EXPLODING DYNAMITE*?

OH, FOR CRYIN' OUT LOUD!

KA-BOOM

WHAT DO WE DO NOW?!

BACK TO HEADQUARTERS!

BUT WE CAN'T GO BACK WITHOUT HER SENSE OF SELF!

YOU WANT US TO GO TO THE *BACK OF THE MIND*?!

IF WE PUT HER SENSE OF SELF BACK, THEN RILEY WILL BE RILEY AGAIN.

TO FIND RILEY'S OLD SENSE OF SELF, THE EMOTIONS WILL HAVE TO GET TO THE STREAM OF CONSCIOUSNESS AND FOLLOW IT TO THE BACK OF THE MIND.

DON'T WORRY. I KNOW RIGHT WHERE THE STREAM IS.

IN LONG-TERM MEMORY, TRYING TO FIND THE STREAM OF CONSCIOUSNESS...

UH, JOY? THIS IS A DEAD END.

EVERYTHING'S CHANGING SO FAST.

I THOUGHT YOU KNEW WHERE YOU WERE GOING!

I DO. I DID... I JUST NEED A MOMENT.

THE LIGHTS COME ON...

RILEY'S *AWAKE!*

SHE'S UP TOO EARLY. WHAT ARE THEY DOING TO HER?!

COME ON, WE'LL FIND ANOTHER WAY!

BACK AT HEADQUARTERS...

WE NEED TO SPEED THINGS UP.

WE NEED RILEY TO BE A FIRE HAWK SO SHE HAS FRIENDS NEXT YEAR.

SO WE HIT THE ICE EARLY AND PRACTICE LIKE NEVER BEFORE.

VERY EARLY MORNING...

"AREN'T WE ALREADY GOOD AT HOCKEY?"

"WE'RE GOOD, BUT THE FIRE HAWKS ARE *GREAT!*"

"THAT'S RIGHT! EVERY TIME WE MISS A SHOT, WE'LL SKATE A LAP."

I SEE I'M NOT THE ONLY ONE WHO LIKES TO START EARLY.

"IT'S VAL! AND WE HAD THE SAME IDEA!"

"WE'RE BASICALLY THE SAME PERSON. WE'RE GONNA BE BEST FRIENDS!"

I TOLD THE OTHER GIRLS YOU'D FIGURE IT OUT. YOU GET WHAT IT TAKES TO BE THE BEST.

"WE SHOULD ASK VAL LOTS OF QUESTIONS. PEOPLE LOVE TALKING ABOUT THEMSELVES!"

SO WHAT WAS YOUR FRESHMAN YEAR ON THE FIRE HAWKS LIKE?

IT WAS A *LOT* OF WORK, BUT IT'S ALSO HOW I MET MY BEST FRIENDS.

"VAL IS SHARING THINGS WITH US!"

A FEW OF US ARE GONNA HANG OUT TONIGHT. *YOU SHOULD COME!*

"OOH! AN EXCLUSIVE INVITATION...WE'RE *GOING!*"

HEY, RILEY.

"WE ARE *NOT* SHARING VAL WITH THEM!"

ANXIETY PLANTS A NEW MEMORY IN RILEY'S BELIEF SYSTEM TO START BUILDING HER NEW SENSE OF SELF. A NEW BELIEF GROWS....

"IF I'M A FIRE HAWK, I WON'T BE ALONE."

MEANWHILE, AT THE STREAM OF CONSCIOUSNESS...

SEE? I TOLD YOU I'D FIND IT!

BUT, JOY--

QUICK, HOP ON SOMETHING! SADNESS, COME ON!

BUT SADNESS POINTS OUT THAT ONE OF THEM NEEDS TO BE AT THE CONSOLE TO BRING THE OTHERS BACK THROUGH A RECALL TUBE--SOMETHING JOY HADN'T THOUGHT OF....

FINE.

SOMEONE'S GONNA HAVE TO CRAWL UP THAT TUBE AND GO BACK TO HEADQUARTERS.

SADNESS, YOU CAN DO IT!

JOY FINDS TWO WALKIE-TALKIES....

WE'LL SIGNAL YOU WHEN WE GET THERE, AND THEN YOU CAN BRING US BACK!

JOY, I CAN'T DO IT. I'M NOT STRONG LIKE YOU.

YOU *ARE* STRONG! I CAN'T GIVE YOU SPECIFIC EXAMPLES RIGHT NOW, BUT *YOU GOT THIS*.

WITH SADNESS ON HER WAY THROUGH A RECALL TUBE AND JOY AND THE OTHERS RIDING DOWN THE STREAM OF CONSCIOUSNESS, RILEY FINISHES PRACTICE...

THERE IT IS. THE RED NOTEBOOK.

EVERYTHING COACH THINKS ABOUT YOU IS IN THERE. THE GOOD AND THE BAD.

WHETHER SHE WANTS YOU ON THE TEAM...

...OR NOT.

YOU GUYS! DON'T FREAK HER OUT.

WHAT? IT'S THE TRUTH.

BACK AT THE STREAM OF CONSCIOUSNESS, THERE'S AN EARTHQUAKE. HELPING ONE ANOTHER, THE EMOTIONS HAVE TO GET OFF THE STREAM FAST....

WHAT HAPPENED?! WHAT IS *THAT*?

THAT'S A *SAR-CHASM.*

SAR-CHASM?

NOW WHAT?! IF WE CAN'T FOLLOW THE *STREAM*, WE DON'T KNOW WHERE WE'RE GOING!

BACK IN THE DORM...

OH YEAH, GET UP AND GLOW IS *SO* AWESOME.

RILEY, WHAT ARE YOU TALKING ABOUT? YOU *LOVE* GET UP AND GLOW.

COME ON, RILEY. WE *JUST* WENT TO THEIR CONCERT.

WELL, YEAH. I MEAN, SURE, BUT--

WE HAD A GREAT TIME.

"GRACE, YOU ARE *NOT* HELPING."

YEAH, WE HAD A *GREAT* TIME.

THE SAR-CHASM KEEPS GETTING BIGGER AS THE EMOTIONS TRY TO FIGURE OUT HOW TO GET ACROSS IT.

88

WHAT ARE WE GONNA DO NOW, JOY?!

WE GO THE LONG WAY, WHICH IS THE BEST WAY!

RILEY CONTINUES TO USE SARCASM....

YEAH, *BEST* NIGHT OF MY LIFE...

WELL, THIS HAS BEEN REALLY FUN.

BUT WE'RE GONNA GO NOW.

OKAY, BYE.

WELL, I'M GONNA CALL IT A NIGHT. IT'S LATE, AND YOU'LL WANNA GET SOME SLEEP BEFORE TOMORROW'S SCRIMMAGE.

WHAT SCRIMMAGE?

TECHNICALLY IT'S NOT YOUR TRYOUT FOR NEXT YEAR, BUT IT BASICALLY IS.

YOU'LL DO GREAT. JUST BE YOURSELF.

DID YOU HEAR THAT?! WE COULD BECOME A *FIRE HAWK* TOMORROW!

BUT HOW DO WE BE OURSELF IF OUR NEW *SELF* ISN'T READY YET?!

EXCELLENT POINT! LET'S MOVE THESE MEMORIES DOWNSTAIRS....

90

BACK AT HEADQUARTERS...

THE *FIRE HAWKS* HAVE ACCEPTED US, *BUT*... IF COACH DOESN'T PUT US ON THE TEAM, NONE OF THAT MATTERS.

EMBARRASSMENT SPOTS SADNESS!

SHHHH...

BUT TO SADNESS' SURPRISE, EMBARRASSMENT HELPS KEEP HER HIDDEN!

ALL RIGHT, GUYS, IT'S GONNA BE A LONG NIGHT.

LET'S GET THE TEAM READY.

MEANWHILE, JOY AND THE OTHERS FOLLOW THE LIGHT FROM RILEY'S SENSE OF SELF AND COME ACROSS IMAGINATION LAND!

FORT PILLOWTON'S STILL HERE! AND IT GOT EVEN BIGGER!

AND IT'S... ORANGE?

JOY AND THE OTHERS FOLLOW THE MIND WORKER...

WE NEED TO HELP RILEY PREPARE.

SEND UP EVERY POSSIBLE THING THAT COULD GO WRONG.

THE MIND WORKERS COME UP WITH EVERY POSSIBLE MISTAKE RILEY COULD MAKE!

THEY'RE USING RILEY'S IMAGINATION AGAINST HER!

WE CAN'T LET HER DO THIS TO RILEY! WE HAVE TO SHUT THIS DOWN.

JOY HAS AN IDEA...SHE DRAWS RILEY SCORING AND EVERYONE HUGGING HER!

DISGUST DRAWS RILEY PAINTING HER NAILS TO MATCH HER JERSEY!

EVERYBODY COPIES HER! SHE IS SO COOL!

WE BUY FLOWERS FOR THE LOSING TEAM!

WHAT? I CAN'T ALWAYS BE THE RAGE GUY.

NAIL POLISH? I'M STARTING TO THINK YOU DON'T UNDERSTAND THE ASSIGNMENT.

WHAT IS GOING ON? WHO'S SENDING UP ALL THIS POSITIVE--

JOY. I KNOW YOU'RE IN THERE.

THE MIND POLICE ARE ON THEIR WAY!

DON'T LISTEN TO *ANXIETY*! SHE'S TRYING TO *CHANGE RILEY*! BUT WE KNOW WHO RILEY IS!

JOY, I'M DOING THIS FOR *YOU*. THIS IS SO RILEY CAN BE HAPPIER.

IF YOU WANTED HER TO BE HAPPY, THEN YOU'D STOP HURTING HER!

WHO'S WITH ME?!

REALLY? NOTHING?

SORRY, JOY.

BUT SLOWLY, THE MOOD CHANGES....

YEAH! A CAT! A LITTLE OFF TOPIC, BUT I'LL TAKE IT!

THE EMOTIONS GRAB HOLD OF A BALLOON...

THEY'RE GETTING AWAY!

BACK AT HEADQUARTERS...

JOY DOESN'T GET IT. WITHOUT OUR PROJECTIONS, WE WON'T BE PREPARED.

I WISH WE KNEW WHAT COACH THOUGHT ABOUT US!

HER NOTEBOOK!

ALL WE GOTTA DO IS SNEAK INTO HER OFFICE AND READ IT.

SHE DOESN'T WANT TO?

ARE WE PUSHING RILEY TOO HARD?

WE GOTTA SEE WHAT'S IN THAT NOTEBOOK! IT'S THE ONLY WAY TO KNOW HOW WE CAN DO BETTER!

ANXIETY RELUCTANTLY CUTS ONE OF RILEY'S BELIEFS...

"FOLLOW THE RULES..."

SNIP

...AND RILEY SNEAKS INTO COACH'S OFFICE!

96

NO, RILEY, DON'T DO IT...

SADNESS SEES ENNUI'S PHONE AND GETS AN IDEA....

WHY DID SHE STOP? SADNESS?

ENNUI, WHERE'S YOUR PHONE?!

OH LA LA, MY PHONE? SERIOUSLY, WHERE IS MY PHONE?!

SADNESS IS HERE SOMEWHERE! *FIND HER!*

SOON SADNESS IS CAUGHT!

I KNOW RILEY SNEAKING AROUND FEELS WRONG, BUT IT'S THE ONLY WAY TO HELP HER.

THIS ISN'T WHO RILEY IS.

IT'S NOT ABOUT WHO RILEY *IS*. IT'S ABOUT WHO SHE NEEDS TO *BE.*

RILEY DECIDES TO LOOK AT THE NOTEBOOK, AND...

"ANDERSEN: *NOT READY YET!*"

WAIT, COACH ALREADY DECIDED?! WE'RE NOT MAKING THE TEAM?

THIS CANNOT BE HAPPENING!

WE'RE GONNA NEED NEW IDEAS.

MEANWHILE, JOY AND THE OTHERS GET CLOSER TO THE BACK OF THE MIND!

WE'RE SO CLOSE, YOU GUYS!

SUDDENLY...

BONK

OW!

OH NO! IT'S A BRAINSTORM!

AS A RESULT OF THE STORM, THE IDEAS--MOST OF THEM BAD--ROLL IN....

THE EMOTIONS CLIMB TO THE TOP OF THE BALLOON....

THE ONLY WAY OUT IS UP. QUICK, GRAB AN IDEA!

IF RILEY TAKES ONE OF THESE BAD IDEAS, IT COULD BE A DISASTER!

THE EMOTIONS JUMP ONTO THE BIG BAD IDEA....

THE IDEA PULLS JOY AND THE OTHERS UP OUT OF THE STORM, AND THEY LET GO JUST BEFORE IT GOES UP THE TUBE TOWARD HEADQUARTERS....

AAAAHHH! HOLD ME! SERIOUSLY, *HOLD ME!*

POOF

YOU HAVE A PARACHUTE?

UH, YES. WHY DON'T ANY OF YOU?

WE'D BETTER GET GOING BEFORE ANXIETY GIVES RILEY ANY OF THOSE BAD IDEAS.

BACK AT HEADQUARTERS...

COACH IS RIGHT. BUT WE'RE SO CLOSE TO A NEW RILEY WHO IS READY.

WE'LL SHOW THEM WE'RE A FIRE HAWK WHO WILL DO WHATEVER IT TAKES.

RILEY DYES SOME OF HER HAIR RED!

"FINALLY! WE'RE ONE OF THEM!"

HEY, ROCKIN' THE RED, HUH?

I HOPE IT'S OKAY. I KNOW I'M NOT OFFICIALLY A FIRE HAWK YET, BUT SINCE WE'RE ON THE SAME TEAM TODAY, WE SHOULD MATCH, RIGHT?

UH, DID YOU *SLEEP* LAST NIGHT?

NO. HOW COULD I? BIG GAME TODAY.

THE SCRIMMAGE STARTS! RILEY IGNORES DANI, WHO IS OPEN FOR A PASS, AND TAKES A SHOT HERSELF AND SCORES....

LEAVE SOME FOR THE REST OF US, HUH?

YES! ONE DOWN! TWO TO GO!

THAT'S RIGHT, COACH. THAT'S *R-I-L-E-Y!* FUTURE FIRE HAWK SUPERSTAR!

MEANWHILE, JOY AND HER FRIENDS CLIMB....

THERE ARE A LOT MORE BAD MEMORIES THAN I REMEMBER SENDING BACK HERE.

THANK GOODNESS THESE AREN'T PART OF HER.

BACK AT THE GAME...

WHAT ARE YOU *DOING*?!

RILEY STEALS THE PUCK FROM HER OWN TEAMMATE, AND...

YES!

RILEY HAS ONLY ONE MORE GOAL TO MAKE, BUT BREE KEEPS BLOCKING HER SHOTS....

COME ON! YOU HAVE TO SCORE!

DETERMINED TO GET THAT THIRD GOAL, RILEY SHOVES GRACE!

WHAM

RILEY SHOOTS, BUT BREE BLOCKS IT AGAIN.

ANDERSEN! PENALTY BOX! TWO MINUTES!

GRACE! ARE YOU OKAY? SHE HIT YOU PRETTY HARD.

"WE HURT GRACE!"

I--I DIDN'T SEE HER.

MEANWHILE, JOY AND THE OTHERS HAVE FOUND RILEY'S OLD SENSE OF SELF, BUT IT'S LOSING STRENGTH!

THERE IT IS!

"I'M A GOOD PERSON."

AFTER ANXIETY PLANTS THE NEWEST MEMORIES INTO THE BELIEF SYSTEM, RILEY'S NEW SENSE OF SELF FORMS, BUT...

"I'M NOT GOOD ENOUGH."

WHAT?

WHY DOES IT SAY THAT?

UM, UH, DON'T WORRY! IT'S JUST THAT SHE KNOWS THERE'S ALWAYS ROOM FOR SELF IMPROVEMENT. SHE'LL BE FINE!

BACK AT HEADQUARTERS...

YOU HAVE TO SCORE, RILEY! OR THIS WILL ALL HAVE BEEN FOR NOTHING!

ANXIETY! YOU'RE PUTTING TOO MUCH PRESSURE ON HER!

ANXIETY CONTINUES TO SPIN OUT OF CONTROL, TRYING TO FIGURE OUT WHAT TO DO.

IN ORDER TO GET RILEY'S SENSE OF SELF BACK TO HEADQUARTERS, ANGER GETS SOME DYNAMITE....

OH, POUCHY!

HI, EVERYBODY! I'M POUCHY!

THE EXPLOSION CAUSES AN AVALANCHE OF BAD MEMORIES THAT THE EMOTIONS RIDE BACK TO RILEY'S BELIEF SYSTEM.

BACK AT HEADQUARTERS...

OH NO! WHAT DID I DO?!

I CAN FIX IT! I CAN FIX IT!

BUT RILEY IS HAVING AN ANXIETY ATTACK!

SKILLS CAMP

RILEY'S PENALTY IS OVER, BUT...

RILEY? ARE YOU OKAY?

COME ON, RILEY! GET IT TOGETHER!

AT LAST, THE EMOTIONS ARRIVE AND THE BAD MEMORIES FLOOD RILEY'S BELIEF SYSTEM, AND NEW BELIEFS START TO GROW....

ANXIETY, WE'VE BOTH DONE THINGS WE THOUGHT WERE BEST FOR RILEY. BUT YOU HAVE TO LET GO.

I JUST WANTED TO HELP RILEY, TO PROTECT HER.

THE EMOTIONS WATCH AS A NEW SENSE OF SELF BEGINS TO FORM....

AS JOY TOUCHES THE CONSOLE, FEELING NEEDED AGAIN, RILEY TAKES A DEEP BREATH...

AND FOR THE FIRST TIME IN A WHILE, RILEY JUST HAS...*FUN!*

I WAS SUCH A JERK TO YOU GUYS. WHEN YOU TOLD ME YOU WERE GOING TO A DIFFERENT SCHOOL, I FREAKED OUT. I'M SO SORRY!

RILEY SHARES A MOMENT WITH THE FIRE HAWKS....

THEY ALL PASS THE PUCK AROUND, LAUGHING AND JOKING.

GREAT WORK THIS WEEKEND! HEY, ANDERSEN--

YES, COACH?

WHEN YOU STARTED OUT THERE, I WASN'T SURE WHAT TO THINK, BUT SOMETHING CHANGED IN THOSE LAST FEW MINUTES. BRING THAT TO TRYOUTS IN THE FALL, OKAY?

THAT'S OUR GIRL!

THE SCHOOL YEAR STARTS, AND RILEY ANXIOUSLY AWAITS THE NEWS....

HOW LONG ARE YOU GOING TO STARE AT YOUR PHONE?

IT'S ALMOST TWO! COACH IS GONNA POST THE LIST ANY MINUTE!

OKAY, TWO PM, THAT'S IN--

SIX MINUTES! WHAT HAPPENS IF WE DON'T BECOME A FIRE HAWK? WELL, THANKS FOR ASKING, JOY. I'LL TELL YOU...

WE DON'T GO PRO. WE HAVE NO FRIENDS AND WE DIE ALONE. AAAHHH!

WE CAN'T CONTROL WHETHER RILEY MAKES THE TEAM.

NO...

BUT EITHER WAY, WE LOVE OUR GIRL. SHE'S GOT THIS.

'CAUSE SHE'S GOT US!

RIGHT?... MAYBE?

ALL RIGHT, EMBARRASSMENT! EVERYBODY LOOK AT EMBARRASSMENT!

I LOVE OUR GIRL.

HOW COULD YOU NOT? SHE'S SUPER SMART.

AND GREAT AT HOCKEY.

SHE'S REALLY CREATIVE.

SHE CAN BE BORED, BUT NEVER BORING.

SHE CAN HAVE REALLY BAD IDEAS.

OCCASIONALLY, SHE CAN EVEN DO THE WRONG THING.

AND SOMETIMES SHE CAN BE TOO HARD ON HERSELF.

BUT EVERY BIT OF RILEY MAKES HER WHO SHE IS. AND WE LOVE ALL OF OUR GIRL.

"EVERY MESSY, BEAUTIFUL PIECE OF HER."

DING

THE END!

107

"A good plan has many parts, Joy."

—Anxiety

INSIDE OUT 2

GRAPHIC NOVEL
SCRIPT ADAPTATION
Steve Behling
LAYOUT
Emilio Urbano
INK
Marco Forcelloni
COLOR
Silvano Scolari,
Maaw Illustration
LETTERS
Chris Dickey
GRAPHIC DESIGN
Chris Dickey

COVER
LAYOUT
Emilio Urbano
INK
Marco Forcelloni
COLOR
Silvano Scolari

DISNEY PUBLISHING WORLDWIDE
Global Magazines,
Comics, and Partworks
PUBLISHER
Lynn Waggoner
EXECUTIVE EDITOR
Carlotta Quattrocolo
EDITORIAL TEAM
Bianca Coletti (Director, Magazines),
Guido Frazzini (Director, Comics),
Stefano Ambrosio (Executive Editor, New
Camilla Vedove (Senior Manager,
Editorial Development),
Behnoosh Khalili (Senior Editor),
Julie Dorris (Senior Editor),
Kendall Tamer (Assistant Editor),
Cristina Casas (Assistant Editor)
DESIGN
Enrico Soave (Senior Designer)
ART
Roberto Santillo (Creative Director),
Stefano Attardi (Illustration Manager)
Marco Ghiglione (Creative Manager)
PORTFOLIO MANAGEMENT
Olivia Ciancarelli (Director)
BUSINESS & MARKETING
Mariantonietta Galla
(Senior Manager, Franchise),
Virpi Korhonen
(Editorial Manager)
CONTRIBUTOR
Simona Grandi
SPECIAL THANKS
Scott Tilley, Nick Balian

3 1901 06154 5002